Matthew and Goliath

Brian Davis

76 pgs.

Illustrations by Ron Wheeler

McRuffy Press

2003

To Ron Wheeler,
Thanks for the extra effort to
make this project possible.

Matthew and Goliath

Published by McRuffy Press
PO Box 212
Raymore, Missouri 64083

Story by Brian Davis
Illustrations by Ron Wheeler
Cover design and illustrations by Ron Wheeler

ISBN 1-59269-058-0

www.McRuffy.com

Contents

1. Nathan Goliath............................ 5

2. The Price of Peace......................13

3. Matthew's New Diet.................. 21

4. Three Smooth Baseballs..............29

5. Blessed Be the Persecuted............37

6. The Headless Choir Member.......44

7. The Flying Giant.........................52

8. The Mystery Box.........................59

9. Citizen of the Month..................68

Chapter 1

Nathan Goliath

Matthew 5:44 But I tell you: Love your enemies and pray for those who persecute you.

Romans 12:14 Bless those who persecute you…

Matthew Day could hear crying as he approached his third grade classroom. The door was closed. He looked at his friends, Rail and Buzz. Rail had a puzzled look on his face.

"What's going on?" asked Buzz as he tried to turn the doorknob. The knob didn't turn.

"We're locked out. I guess we should all go home. Let's start our three day weekend."

Buzz was the class clown. He never missed an opportunity to joke around. It was typical of him to miss the fact that someone behind the door was upset.

"You have no business in there," said the school nurse. She had just walked up behind them. She was carrying an ice pack.

"I was just going to get my spelling book," said Buzz. He was always quick with an excuse.

"You could certainly use the extra study time," said the nurse.

Buzz looked puzzled. How could she know? The nurse saw the surprised look on the boy's face.

"I am the school nurse," she explained. "And your spelling grade is not too healthy."

Matthew and Rail laughed. The nurse unlocked the door. She slipped inside without opening the door all the way. Buzz tried to follow her.

"O-u-t, out!" spelled the nurse with her finger pointed at Buzz.

"Isn't out spelled o-w-t?" asked Buzz. He saw the stern look on her face. "Just kidding," said Buzz as he backed out of the doorway.

More classmates gathered around the door. School was about to start. The hallway was getting noisier. Buzz put his ear to the door.

"Get quiet," yelled Buzz. "I can't tell what they're saying."

Mrs. Anderson, their teacher, opened the door. "I can certainly hear what you're saying, Bradley." Bradley was Buzz's real name. "Now clear a path and let us through."

The crowd around the door moved back. They parted like Moses parted the Red Sea. Everyone watched as the teacher, the nurse, and Stacy Lane walked out of the classroom. Stacy was one of Matthew's classmates. She was holding a bag of ice over her right eye.

A murmur rose from the crowd. This had to

be serious. At least Stacy was walking, thought Matthew. But, everyone had more questions than answers.

"I'll be back in a moment," said Mrs. Anderson. "Everyone go find your seats and begin your morning board work."

Mrs. Anderson always had something

written for them to do on the chalkboard. Buzz started to go in. All of the sudden he stopped.

"I'd rather wait out here," said Buzz.

Matthew looked over his shoulder. Only one person was in the room. It was Nathan Goliath. He was the biggest third grader Matthew had ever seen. This was Nathan's second day at Matthew's school.

Matthew thought Nathan was trouble the first time he saw him. He shuddered as he thought about it. What had the giant third grader done to Stacy's eye?

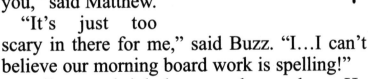

"I don't blame you," said Matthew.

"It's just too scary in there for me," said Buzz. "I...I can't believe our morning board work is spelling!"

Rail stepped right between the two boys. He put his lunchbox on the shelf. Rail calmly hung his backpack on a hook. He unzipped it and pulled out his folders. Matthew wasn't surprised. Rail was smaller than the other students, but he was fearless.

By now all the students had crowded just

inside the door. They wanted to see what Nathan would do to Rail. They both sat in the same row by the windows. Nathan was in back, course. He had to be. No other third grader could see around him.

Rail was in the front. He had to be. He couldn't see around any of the other students. Matthew sat in the next row, second desk back. They were still close enough to talk when the teacher let them. It was a near perfect seating arrangement, until yesterday.

Just as Rail walked by Nathan's desk, he tripped. Rail landed flat on his face. His folders slid across the classroom. The boys and girls in the classroom jumped back.

Nathan didn't seem to notice. He was staring out the window. The big third grader had a giant smile on his face. He even started waving to someone outside.

Matthew was getting angry. The new boy had just tripped his best friend. Nathan seemed to be very pleased with the mess he created. Then, Matthew noticed Nathan was waving to someone.

It was Stacy. She was walking out of the school with her mother. Matthew grew angrier. How could this huge kid be so cruel? Nathan's waving seemed to mock her. There was even a proud look on his face.

None of the other third graders rushed to help Rail. They were afraid of Nathan. Matthew was so stunned he didn't think of helping his friend at first. Then he realized that Rail needed him.

Matthew rushed over to him. He was careful to stay away from Nathan as much as possible. Rail seemed to be ok. He was more embarrassed than hurt. Matthew helped gather and sort the folders and papers.

Suddenly, Nathan turned around. "You should be more careful," Nathan warned. "You don't want to end up like Stacy."

"Uh…no sir," stammered Rail.

"I'll be careful too," said Matthew.

"That's a good idea," said Nathan. "There seems to be a lot of accidents happening around here." Then Nathan smiled.

Matthew and Rail scurried to their desks. The two boys peeked over their shoulders. Nathan was staring at Rail. Now the huge third grader had a big frown on his face. Matthew thought it was one of the meanest looks he had ever seen

on a third grader. A cold chill ran down his spine. He glanced at Rail. He looked a little pale and swallowed hard.

It had been such a great year up until now, thought Matthew. Why did this bully have to join their classroom? Matthew watched as the other children quietly took their seats. Nobody even looked at Nathan Goliath. The students in the rows around him were careful to walk around his desk.

Chapter 2

The Price of Peace

Mrs. Anderson seemed to be in a good mood when she came back to the classroom. The students didn't even notice her return. They were all busy doing the morning board work. Everyone was so afraid of Nathan. The normal distracting chatter between students was missing. There was nothing else to do but school work.

Still, Matthew was surprised that Mrs. Anderson didn't say something about Stacy. Why wasn't Nathan being punished? Matthew wondered if even Mrs. Anderson was afraid of Nathan. He was almost bigger than the teacher.

Trudy Upton, Stacy's best friend, raised her hand.

"Yes, Trudy," said Mrs. Anderson.

"Is Stacy going to be alright?" asked Trudy.

"She'll be fine. I'm sure she'll be here Monday," said Mrs. Anderson.

"I hope the rest of us make it through the

day," said Buzz. "There seem to be a lot of 'accidents' happening in this classroom."

Everyone turned and looked at Nathan. The big third grader smiled.

"I'll be careful," said Nathan. "I hope everyone else will be careful too."

Everyone quickly turned around. All the students worked quietly that morning. Soon it was time for morning recess. The class was afraid of what Nathan might do to them on the playground.

"Ok class, put away your work. It's time for recess," said Mrs. Anderson.

Buzz raised his hand, "May I stay in to study my spelling?"

Mrs. Anderson laughed, "Quit joking around, Buzz."

Ten other hands shot up. "Can I stay in, too?" everyone was asking.

"I must have the funniest class," said Mrs. Anderson. "I want everyone to line up, except Nathan."

"Except Nathan?" said Matthew. "I'm ready for recess!"

A line formed very quickly at the door. They waited for Mr. Morgan's class to pass. Then Mrs. Anderson's class followed behind. Mr. Morgan had recess duty that day. Four third grade classes had recess at the same time.

Mrs. Anderson's class was relieved to get outside. They all talked about what had happened to Stacy and Rail. Soon, all the third graders knew about the giant in Mrs.

Anderson's class. They were all glad Nathan had to sit out this recess.

Then it happened. The door to the school building opened. Out stepped the biggest third grader in all of the classes. He was even bigger than a lot of the fifth graders. Nathan Goliath seemed to fill the whole doorway.

"What do you suppose happened to Mrs. Anderson?" asked Trudy Upton.

"I don't know, but I'm really going to miss her," said Buzz.

"Stop it," said Matthew. "I'm sure there's a good reason he's out here."

"Nobody ever misses just part of a recess," said Rail. "Especially when you give someone a black eye."

"Something doesn't make sense here," said Matthew. He started walking toward Nathan.

"Come back," yelled Buzz. "It's not worth the risk!"

Matthew stopped. He was close enough to hear what Nathan was saying. The boy towered over another group of third graders. Matthew could see the fear in their eyes.

"I'm collecting money..," said Nathan.

All the students pulled out coins. They handed them to Nathan.

"Is this enough?" asked one of the boys. "I

can bring more money Monday."

"Okay," said Nathan. "I'll look for you Monday at recess."

The students ran off. Matthew watched Nathan count the money. Nathan put it in his pocket. Rail, Buzz, and Trudy ran up to Matthew.

"What happened?" asked Rail.

"He took some money from those kids," said Matthew.

Nathan looked at Matthew, Rail, Buzz, and Trudy. He seemed to be watching them. Matthew had a sinking feeling in his stomach.

"Good-bye allowance," Matthew said as he reached for the change in his pocket.

"Oh no," said Rail. "I don't have any money."

"Why don't you run to Mr. Morgan?" said Matthew.

"And tell on Nathan?" asked Rail.

"Are you crazy?" asked Buzz. "You'll really make Nathan mad if you tell on him. Besides, I don't want to see Mr. Morgan get hurt."

"No," said Matthew. "Don't tell on Nathan. Just hide from him. He won't pick on you if you're standing by a teacher."

"Why don't we all run?" asked Buzz.

"Because we have to face Nathan

sometime," explained Matthew. "We can't run all the time. Besides, I have some money. I'll give him some money for Rail, too. But, Rail you better run just in case."

"In case of what?" asked Rail.

"In case I don't have enough money to satisfy Nathan," answered Matthew.

Rail ran over to the four-square game Mr. Morgan was refereeing. Rail got in line to take a turn. That way it didn't look like he was hiding out. But, Rail watched his three brave friends. Nathan was talking to them now. Rail was too far away to hear what was being said.

"Do you have any money for Rail?" asked Nathan. "I'm…"

Matthew interrupted him, "We know what you're doing. I hope I have enough." Matthew reached in his pocket. He pulled out two quarters, a dime, and four pennies.

"That's very kind of you," said Nathan. "What about you two?" He asked Buzz and Trudy.

Trudy was about to say, "You wouldn't hit a girl." Then she remembered Stacy's black eye. She reached into her pocket and pulled out a crisp one dollar bill.

Buzz only had eighteen cents. He had just bought a new joke book. Buzz handed Nathan the dime, nickel, and three pennies. Buzz knew it wasn't much. He closed his eyes and waited for the punch.

"Thanks," said Nathan as he walked off to another group of children.

Buzz opened one eye, "Is he gone?"

"Yes," answered Matthew.

"At least he's an inexpensive bully," said

Buzz. "It only cost me eighteen cents to not get punched."

"Cheap! I paid him a whole dollar," said Trudy.

"Maybe it just cost more to not be mean to girls," said Buzz.

"I'm just glad it's Friday," said Matthew. "I don't have enough money for another recess."

By the time Mr. Morgan blew the whistle, Nathan had two pockets stuffed with money. He was the only third grader with a smile on his face. Every student now knew who the huge boy was. They all wondered how they would make it through the next week.

"He can't beat us all up," Matthew said to Rail as they walked to the line.

"I wonder if he'll just take turns," said Rail. "It would be pretty tiring fighting all the kids that don't have money."

"I wonder what I could sell to raise some money?" said Trudy.

"Maybe I could sell my spelling book," Buzz smiled. "Having a bully around may not be so bad after all."

Chapter 3

Matthew's New Diet

Clouds moved in over the next hour. Matthew watched the big raindrops pelt the windows. He had never been so glad to see rain before. This would cancel the after lunch recess.

Now he could eat in peace. That nervous feeling turned into a hungry feeling. The teacher always called rows to line up for lunch. Rail's row was the first one called.

Students buying hot lunch formed one line at the door. The rest walked to the coat rack and shelf. Lunch boxes lined the shelves.

It was normally like that every other Friday. Most of the students brought their lunch. It was tuna fish day. Only Rail ate the hot lunch everyday. He seemed to be grateful no matter what they had for lunch.

Matthew watched and waited as the first row grabbed their lunches. He especially kept his eye on Nathan. That wasn't too tough. Nathan was so big it was hard to see anyone else. Still, he wasn't prepared for what happened next.

Nathan reached out for the red lunchbox. It was a red Super Squid Master Detective lunchbox. Matthew almost jumped out of his seat. He was about to yell, "That's my lunchbox!" Then he remembered how big Nathan was.

Still, he wasn't taking this lying down. Matthew's row was called next. He got in line behind Nathan. Nathan turned around. He noticed Matthew looking at the box.

"Do you like my new lunchbox?" asked Nathan. He had a big smile on his face. "Where's your lunch?"

Matthew felt that Nathan was just being mean. How could he be so cruel? Matthew's face was turning red. If only Nathan wasn't so big.

"Where's your lunch, Matt?" asked Mrs. Anderson.

"It's uh…" Matthew glanced at Nathan.

Nathan just smiled back. He patted the Super Squid Master Detective lunchbox. It was the greatest lunchbox ever made, thought Matthew. It also contained something other than tuna fish.

"Why don't you get in the hot lunch line," said Mrs. Anderson. "I'll send a charge slip home. You can bring the money to pay for it Monday."

Matthew sighed. He hated tuna fish. He also hated starving. Then he thought of something else he hated, bringing money to school.

"Can my parents mail the money?" asked Matthew.

"I guess they can," answered Mrs. Anderson. "But, they don't need to do that."

"Oh, they need to," interrupted Buzz. "If the school wants the money, it will have to be mailed."

"I'm not sure I understand," said Mrs. Anderson. "Do you want to explain?" she asked Matthew.

Matthew glanced at Nathan. He didn't believe the lunch money would make it to the classroom. Not in Matthew's pocket anyway.

Matt could just picture Nathan waiting in some dark corner of the hallway Monday morning. The giant would be waiting to take the lunch money. Matthew would be Nathan's first victim of the week.

"Uh…my parents need to pay by check…in the mail," stammered Matthew. "It's for their taxes."

"Hmmm," Mrs. Anderson rubbed her chin. "I guess that would be fine. Just line up behind Rail."

The class marched down to the lunchroom. Rail and Matthew ate as far away from Nathan as possible. Actually, Matthew didn't eat. He was too angry to eat. He also didn't like the food.

Matthew watched Nathan at the next table enjoying the contents of the Super Squid Master Detective lunchbox. His mom must have packed a special lunch. The food looked better than ever. Every bite Nathan took made Matthew angrier.

 "Are you going to eat your tuna?" asked Rail.

"You can have it," said Matthew, "if you help me out."

"What are you going to do?" asked Rail.

"I'm getting my lunch back!" Matthew gritted his teeth. "I don't care how big Nathan Goliath is!"

"You're going to just walk up and take it? I can't let you do that. I'd miss you too much. You can keep the tuna fish sandwich."

"All you need to do is distract him," explained Matthew. "I'll do the rest. Nathan won't even know who took the food."

"But it's almost all gone. He's about ready for that cupcake," pleaded Rail.

"It's the principle of the thing," explained Matt. "Besides, I love cupcakes."

Rail sighed. "What do you want me to do?"

"Just distract him," answered Matthew.

"How will I do that?"

"Just talk to him," said Matthew.

"Talk to him? About what?" asked Rail.

"I don't know. Ask him how he got so big. Just do something. We're running out of time."

"And food," said Rail. Nathan was gnawing

on the core of a sweet, red apple.

Rail stood up. He took a deep breath. Rail walked to the other table. Just as he got there he tripped and fell.

Rail was face to toe with the biggest shoe he had ever seen on a third grader. Nathan leaned down under the table. The boy had a huge grin on his face.

"Did you lose something?" asked Nathan.

Matthew saw his chance. He hopped from his seat and made a dash for the Super Squid Master Detective lunchbox. Matthew snatched the cupcake and ran out the cafeteria door. He stopped in the hallway.

Matthew stuffed his face with the cupcake. It was the best tasting cupcake he had ever eaten. It was just what he needed to make it through the rest of the day. Matthew glanced back into the cafeteria.

Nathan was looking all around his table for the cupcake. That made the chocolate desert seem even better to Matthew. It was the sweet taste of revenge. Matthew was rather proud of himself.

He smiled as he walked back into the cafeteria. Matt had stood up to the bully. He had reclaimed his food. Matthew was feeling braver than he had all day.

"Looking for something?" asked Matthew as he walked by Nathan.

"Yes," answered Nathan as he continued looking down at the table. "I'm looking for a chocolate cup..." Nathan stopped when he looked up.

"Cake," Matthew finished the sentence. "A cupcake? Hmm, I saw it here just a minute ago. Maybe someone took it. There's been a lot of lunches coming up missing today."

Matthew strutted back to his seat. Nathan was still watching him. Rail was busy eating Matthew's tuna fish sandwich. He finally glanced at Matthew. Rail's mouth dropped open.

"Rail," said Matthew. "Close your mouth. I don't like looking at half-chewed tuna sandwiches. Want to hear something funny?" asked Matthew. "Nathan has no idea what happened to the cupcake. He's looking all over for it."

"I...I think he knows where it went," stuttered Rail.

"How could he?" asked Matthew.

"Your face is covered with chocolate icing," answered Rail.

Chapter 4

Three Smooth Baseballs

Matthew didn't feel so good after lunch. He felt like he was going to have a headache. Well, at least he thought his head would ache. He could just imagine Nathan's fist meeting his face.

There was only one thing to do. Matthew needed to go home early. It was a matter of survival. Matthew didn't like to pretend he was sick. He didn't like to lie. Matt didn't have to do either one. He was so nervous, he really felt sick.

A half-hour later, he was home. Mrs. Day brought him a cup of warm soup. She took the thermometer out of Matthew's mouth. Mrs. Day held it up.

"You don't have a fever," she said.

"I think it was something I ate," answered Matthew remembering the cupcake.

"Well, you'll be up and around in no time," said Mrs. Day. "It's supposed to be a nice day tomorrow. I'm sure you'll want to play baseball."

Baseball, without Nathan. No school, no Nathan, no problem. That was the cure that Matthew was looking for. He felt great the next morning.

After breakfast, Matthew jogged to the baseball field. It was right behind the church his family attended. Several kids were already there. Team captains had been chosen.

"You made it!" said Rail when he saw Matt. "I thought you might be too sick to play. You can be on my team." Rail was one of the captains.

He liked to volunteer to be captain. That way he wouldn't be picked last. Although Rail wasn't that good of a player, he was a really good captain. Some of the players would argue over playing different positions.

Rail was gifted in solving those kinds of problems. He would point out the good things he saw in the players. He would tell them why they were better playing in different positions.

Plus, he always let the other players bat before him. He played whatever position no one else wanted to play. But, he always picked Matthew first. Of course, Matthew was picked last this time. He had almost missed the start of the game.

Now, Rail's team had one more player than the other team. "You can have the next player that shows up," offered Rail.

There were always kids who came late. That's because there really wasn't an official starting time. The game started when there were enough players to play. The game always began with a coin toss.

Rail called tails. The shiny quarter landed heads side up. Rail's team would bat last. The boys on the other team cheered. Every team always wanted to bat first.

Rail told Matthew to pitch. He always let Matthew pitch. The other kids didn't mind. Matthew was a good pitcher. The most important thing about being the pitcher is being able to throw the ball over the plate. Games get kind of boring after twenty or thirty walks.

The game was just about to start. Matthew had just thrown a warm-up pitch. That's when it happened. He noticed the looks on faces of the other team. They were all watching something.

Matthew had a sinking feeling that he knew what it was. He slowly turned around. Matthew groaned. Walking toward the baseball field was the biggest third grader any of them had ever seen. Nathan Goliath had a baseball glove on his hand, a bat on his shoulder, and a big smile on his face.

The other team captain yelled out, "You're on our team."

"I'm glad he's on our side," said one of the boys.

"What's your name?" asked the captain.

"Nathan Goliath."

"You can bat first," said the captain.

"Thanks," said Nathan.

He tossed down his glove. Nathan strolled to the plate. The catcher backed up against the fence. He wanted to give Nathan as much room as possible.

Nathan had a huge bat. He took a few practice swings. Matthew thought it actually stirred up a breeze. The leaves on the trees rustled. Matthew began to have that sick feeling from the day before.

"I'm not afraid," Matthew told himself. But, he didn't believe himself. He was afraid. He felt so small and weak compared to Nathan.

Then Matthew thought of David and Goliath in the Bible. David stood up to a giant that was trying to kill him. Nathan just wanted to hit a baseball. At least that's what Matthew hoped. Matthew tossed the other two practice baseballs to the dugout.

Matthew slapped the remaining baseball in his glove. "I'll show him. He's not getting a hit off of me!" he mumbled to himself. He didn't say it loudly. He didn't want Nathan to hear.

He decided to throw the ball harder than he had ever thrown it before. He wanted to let Nathan Goliath know that he couldn't be pushed around. Matthew remembered the bravery of David.

Matthew went into his wind-up. He released the ball. Matthew threw it so hard, he almost fell over. The ball zoomed toward the plate. It was the hardest, fastest pitch Matthew had ever thrown.

It was also the wildest. Nathan couldn't swing. He couldn't even move, until it was too late. The baseball smacked him right in the forehead. Nathan looked like a Giant Redwood tree that had just been chopped down.

He fell flat on his back. Dust rose from the batter's box. Matthew thought he felt the ground shake. Everyone was stunned, everyone, except Nathan. He was completely still. The baseball had knocked him out.

The new pastor at the church had seen the whole thing. He ran over. Nathan was starting to wake up. His giant hand was rubbing his forehead. The pastor helped him to his feet and led him to the church.

The other boys didn't follow. They just

watched. Matthew watched the closest. He noticed something the other boys didn't. There was a dusty streak down Nathan's face. Matthew thought he saw tears.

Matthew didn't know how he felt. Suddenly, Nathan looked weak and…well…human. He had never thought of Nathan as someone who had feelings. Some of the kids who lost money the day before came up to Matthew.

"You showed him!" smiled Buzz. "He won't mess with us again!"

"He had it coming," said another. "You're a hero, Matt."

Matthew wasn't so sure. He didn't feel like a hero. He just felt tired. The slaying of the giant ended the baseball game before it really began.

At least for Matthew it did. He told the others he didn't feel well. They thought he just felt sick from the day before. Matthew knew differently.

Chapter 5

Blessed Be the Persecuted

"That was a quick ballgame," said Matt's father as Matthew came in the kitchen door. Then he saw the look on Matt's face. "Are you feeling alright?" He put his hand on Matthew's forehead. "Don't feel too warm."

"I don't feel well, but it's not that kind of sick," answered Matthew. "I...I may have hurt someone. Not too badly. I mean, they didn't need an ambulance or anything."

Mr. Day could tell it wasn't an emergency. Matthew would have come running into the house. He didn't. So, Mr. Day pulled out a chair at the kitchen table.

He motioned with his hand, "Step into my office."

Matthew sat down. Mr. Day pulled out another chair. He could tell that Matthew was feeling guilty.

"Tell me what happened."

"I was pitching. I hit a player in the head," explained Matthew.

"Does an adult know about this?" asked his father.

"Yes. The new pastor led the boy to the church," answered Matthew. "The boy seemed okay. He was walking and everything. But, I think he was crying."

"That would be natural if he were hurt. That's a good sign. I mean, he could have been knocked out," said Mr. Day.

"I think it did knock him out. But, he woke up," said Matthew.

Matthew's father could see how terrible

Matthew felt. "It was an accident. That happens sometimes when you play."

Matthew sighed, "I'm not sure it was an accident."

"Not sure?"

"Well," explained Matthew. "I don't like this boy very much."

"I thought you liked all the kids in the neighborhood. Who don't you like?" asked Mr. Day.

"It's a new boy. His name is Nathan. He's in my class. Nathan is the biggest third grader I've ever seen. He's a big bully."

"A bully?"

"He's only been going to our school two days," explained Matthew. "So far he's given Stacy a black eye. He tripped Rail twice. Nathan took all my money.

He took money from a lot of third graders at recess. Then, he stole my Super Squid Master Detective lunch box, before lunch. I had to eat tuna."

"Did anyone tell a teacher?" asked Mr. Day.

"Who wants to be a tattletale? Besides, every one is afraid of him. I just didn't like him being mean to everyone.

Then, he came to the baseball game. I was afraid he was going to hurt someone. I really didn't want that someone to be me."

"So, you threw the baseball at his head?" Mr. Day looked worried.

"That's what I'm not sure about," said Matthew. "I just threw it as hard as I could. I keep telling myself I was really trying to throw a strike. But…" Matthew paused.

Mr. Day leaned forward, "But, what?"

"I…I was glad I hit him," said Matthew. "Then, I saw the pastor being nice to him. I also think Nathan was crying."

Mr. Day patted Matthew on the hand, "And all of the sudden, this boy didn't seem so tough. You felt sorry for him. That's called compassion."

"That's right," said Matthew. "I know Nathan deserved to be taught a lesson. All the other boys were happy when Nathan got hit.

I feel so bad about it now. I had imagined all kinds of ways to get even with Nathan. It always seemed right when I thought about it."

"So, maybe I did hit him on purpose," said Matthew. "But, I wish I had never played baseball, ever…"

Matthew's father knew how Matthew loved to play baseball. "I think it was an accident. But, you're feeling guilty because you were happy about it. You're not used to hurting people. I'm glad it bothers you to hurt others. It shows you're a caring person."

"But, hurting someone doesn't help. The Bible tells us to bless those who persecute us. If Nathan is being mean to you, he's persecuting you. Being kind to mean people helps them to change," explained Mr. Day.

"I did bless Nathan with my sixty-four cents. He also blessed himself with my lunch. I've been a great blessing to him," explained Matthew. "I even blessed him with my fast ball."

"I'm not sure that's what the Bible means…" Mr. Day started to explain.

"If he learns not to pick on people, won't that bless Nathan?" asked Matthew. "Maybe then he could make some friends. That must be why I felt happy about hitting him. I was just being a good Christian."

"I don't think it works that way. In a way, you also persecuted Nathan," Mr. Day tried to explain.

"That's great. If I persecuted Nathan, I'll be blessed, too," Matt reasoned.

Matthew jumped up from the table. He gave his dad a hug. "Thanks for talking with me. I feel much better. I now know I did the right thing. I'm ready to play some baseball!"

Matthew ran out the door. He almost ran over his mother. She was carrying three sacks of groceries. She was going to ask him to help, but Matthew was too fast. He had grabbed his baseball glove and was running to the park.

"What happened to him?" asked Mrs. Day.

"He was upset. We had a little talk," explained Mr. Day.

"It must have worked. He's not upset now," said Mrs. Day. "Anyway, can you help me unload the car?"

"Sure. I'll even cook lunch," offered Mr. Day.

"I've had your cooking before," said Mrs. Day. "And I didn't buy any frozen pizzas. So, just unloading the groceries is enough. Why would you want to cook lunch?"

"Well," explained Mr. Day, "The Bible says to bless those who persecute us. If you ate my cooking you would feel persecuted. Then, you would have to bless me. You do believe in the Bible, don't you?"

Mrs. Day laughed. "First of all, I wouldn't eat your cooking. You would have to take me out to lunch. Then, I would be blessed."

"And I would feel persecuted," added Mr. Day.

Mrs. Day shook her head, "Sometimes you think just like Matthew."

Chapter 6

The Headless Choir Member

Matthew's older sister, Rachel, was the first one ready for church. She wasn't like other girls who spent hours in the bathroom. That always frustrated Matthew. She was always out in plenty of time for Matthew to take a bath.

"Why can't I have a normal sister?" Matthew grumbled as he headed for the tub.

"Don't make us late," warned Rachel. "We have to sing in the choir this morning."

"I have to take a bath and listen to you sing all in one morning. Now I know what it's like to be very persecuted," answered Matthew.

Some mornings he could be pretty grumpy. This was one of them. Then a thought struck him. Persecuted!

Sunday would be a day without Nathan. It would be a day without Goliath's persecution. Suddenly, Matthew felt very cheerful.

This was a special day at church. It was the first Sunday for the new pastor. Their last pastor had just retired. He and his wife moved to another state to be near their grandchildren.

The Day family decided to walk to church. It was a beautiful day. It was the kind of day that just made you feel happy inside.

Matthew was especially excited. His father told him the pastor had a son his age. Maybe, Matthew would meet a new friend.

As soon as they got to church, Matthew and Rachel went to the choir room. The children's choir got to come in a special door. It was at the front of the church. Matthew didn't mind being in the choir.

He thought it was kind of fun. The choir got to come into the service late. Sometimes they missed the first fifteen minutes of church. What Matthew thought was the most fun was sitting at the front of the church.

He could tell who was awake and who was

sleeping. He liked the expressions on the faces of the men. Their wives would poke them. The husbands would jump.

Then they would pretend they were never asleep. But, at the same time, Matthew's parents could see him giggling. So, he would get in trouble every week the Children's Choir sang.

"Matthew," said Mrs. Clark, the choir director. "Would you take this music out to the piano?"

"Sure," said Matthew. It made him feel important to help out Mrs. Clark.

"Good," said Mrs. Clark. "When you get back, we'll practice your solo."

Solo! Matthew had forgotten all about it. He was going to be singing in front of everyone. He would have to sing all alone. Matthew began to feel butterflies in his stomach.

Matthew walked out to the piano. He saw his parents were sitting in their usual spot. They sat three rows back, right in front of the choir. They said it was because they liked to hear Rachel and Matthew sing. Matthew knew it was also so they could keep an eye on him.

He was walking back to the little door up on the platform. All of the sudden his jaw dropped. The new pastor had just walked in. But, that's not what surprised him. Right behind the pastor was Nathan Goliath. Nathan had a big black eye.

Matthew ducked down behind some chairs. He crawled back to the door. Matthew pushed it open. He was safe in the choir room.

"Did you see that?" Mrs. Jones asked Matthew's mother. She was sitting in the fourth row.

"What?" asked Mrs. Day.

"That door just opened by itself," said Mrs. Jones. "You don't think the church is haunted?"

Mrs. Day laughed. "Sure, it's probably the headless choir member," she teased.

Meanwhile, Matthew had made it safely back to the choir room. He didn't think Nathan saw him. He was still crawling along the floor. Mrs. Clark knelt down to him.

"Why are you lying down? Are you not feeling well? Your mother told me you had been sick. Maybe you should go sit with your parents," said Mrs. Clark.

"Maybe you're right," said Matthew as he stood up.

He opened the door. Matthew saw his parents. He also saw Nathan. The giant third grader was sitting on the front row. Mrs. Jones was introducing herself. There was no way Matthew could get to his parents without walking past Nathan.

"I think I'll stay here," said Matthew.

Surely, Nathan wouldn't try to hit him while he was singing. Still, Matthew would have to get out of the church without Nathan catching

him. He would have to sneak out.

What he needed was a disguise. He looked around the choir room. There wasn't much for disguises. Matthew would have to be creative.

The church service began with everyone singing a song. The Children's Choir waited in back. All the people stood while they sang.

Next, the new pastor walked to the front of the church. He stepped up to a microphone. It squealed when he turned it on.

"I'd like to welcome any visitors this morning," said the pastor. "If this is your first time here, I know how you feel. It's my first time here, too." Everyone laughed.

"At least you don't have to preach," he continued. "My wife tells me that I better stay awake during the sermon this week. I don't want to make a bad first impression." The people laughed even harder.

"Who's the boy on the front row?" Mr. Day whispered to Mrs. Day.

"That's the pastor's son," Mrs. Day whispered to Mr. Day. "He's in Matthew's class. His name is Nathan."

"That's Nathan?" whispered Mr. Day to his wife. "The Nathan?" he said more loudly.

"Shh…" said Mrs. Day. "The choir is about to sing."

The Children's Choir came out the narrow door. Mrs. Clark led the way. Matthew made sure he was last. He would have stayed in there.

On most mornings he could have gotten away with it. But, this morning he had a solo. Suddenly, Matthew had an idea.

The choir sang its first song. Then, they sang the first verse of the next song. It had Matthew's solo part in the middle. Matthew slipped through the door. The choir was still standing. He hid behind Rachel.

The choir would sit down. Matthew would stay standing and sing his solo. At least, that was the way it was planned. Just as Matthew opened his mouth, Mrs. Jones screamed.

"The headless choir member!" she shouted right before she fainted.

Matthew had pulled the choir robe above his head. He was just hiding his face from Nathan. But, Mrs. Jones was right. Matthew looked just like a headless choir member.

The screaming and fainting caused a great stir in the church. Everyone gathered around Mrs. Jones. Matthew saw his chance. He threw off the robe, ran down the aisle, and out the door.

Chapter 7

The Flying Giant

Matthew looked out the window. His parents and Rachel were coming up the sidewalk. Matthew could tell his parents were upset. He expected them to be upset.

They didn't come home from church right away. It seems nobody noticed that Matthew had left. Everyone was paying attention to Mrs. Jones.

Mrs. Clark had ushered all the children off to Sunday school. His parents just thought

Matthew was with them. After church, Rachel told them that Matthew had skipped Sunday school. Matthew couldn't imagine how much trouble he was in. But, he had thought about it a lot over the last hour.

He wanted to run away and hide. But, there was no use. Where would he go? Besides, it was almost lunchtime. He was getting hungry.

The door opened. Matthew braced himself to be yelled at. His mother was the first through the door.

She was followed by Rachel. Finally, his father came into the house. He looked the most upset.

"Oh good, you're safe," said Mrs. Day. She gave him a little kiss on the forehead. Then she walked off to the kitchen.

"How's my Matty boy holding up?" asked his father. "That was some solo." He ruffled Matthew's hair as he walked by. He followed Mrs. Day and kept talking to her.

"What a solo! It was so low we couldn't even see your head," Rachel said to Matthew. She went up the stairs to change clothes. "And, Mrs. Jones still thinks she saw a headless choir member," she yelled back.

Matthew followed his parents into the kitchen. Matthew's dad pointed at him.

"That's exactly what I mean," said Mr. Day to Mrs. Day. "That big bully has made going to church frightening."

"Who me?" said Matthew. "I didn't mean to frighten anyone."

"Not you," said Mrs. Day. "Nathan Goliath, the pastor's son."

"So, you're upset because he's a big bully?" asked Matthew.

"No, we're upset with his dad," answered Mr. Day.

"Did he pick on you too? Did he take our lunch money? Is that why we're eating at home?" Matthew was starting to get angry.

He could just picture Nathan and his dad with offering plates. He pictured them walking up and down isles. He imagined frightened old ladies giving them all their money. Nathan and his dad would just smile at all that money.

"No, nothing like that," said Matthew's mother.

"It was his sermon," explained his father.

"Did it keep you awake?" asked Matthew.

Matthew's mother laughed.

"No," answered his father.

"So, you did fall asleep?" asked Matthew.

"I mean no, that's not why I'm upset. I didn't like what he talked about," explained Mr. Day.

"Well, it was from the Bible," said Mrs. Day. "Everything he said was true."

"Yes, but he's the wrong person to talk about it!" answered Mr. Day.

"Talk about what?" asked Matthew.

"Blessing those who persecute you, being nice to people who aren't nice to you," said Matthew's father.

"Isn't that what you told me yesterday?" asked Matthew. "When you explained to me that I was blessing Nathan when I hit him."

Mrs. Day frowned at Mr. Day.

"I didn't say that. Anyway, I know it's true that we should bless those who persecute us. Yet, from Pastor Goliath, it sounds like he's saying we should let his son get away with being a bully."

"Maybe he doesn't know his son is a bully," suggested Mrs. Day. "You should call the pastor and talk to him."

"I have a better idea," said Mr. Day. "I'll go right over to the church and talk to the pastor in person."

Mr. Day left the house and walked toward the church. Matthew followed him from a distance. He didn't want his father to see him. Matthew didn't want to be told to stay home.

Matthew was glad he followed. His father needed a witness. Matthew saw it all. In fact, he was the only one who saw what happened. His father was so upset, he wasn't really paying attention.

Mr. Day was walking across the yard to the pastor's house. It was right next to the church. That's when it happened. Matthew couldn't believe his eyes.

Nathan Goliath came flying through the air. He tackled Mr. Day. Matthew watched his father fall under the weight of the giant third grader. Mr. Day was stunned.

Nathan ran to his house. Matthew ran to his father. Mr. Day was just trying to stand. Matthew knew he needed to act quickly. He didn't want to be around if Nathan came back.

Matthew helped his dazed father out of the pastor's yard. They walked to the park. Matthew and his father sat down on a park bench. It was behind some tall bushes. Matthew knew Nathan wouldn't be able to see them.

"What happened?" asked Mr. Day.

"Nathan attacked you," said Matthew. "He just flew through the air and knocked you down. It's a good thing I followed you. I knew there might be trouble."

Mr. Day rubbed his jaw. "It feels like he punched me."

"It looked like he punched you," said Matthew.

"Well, let's go home," said Mr. Day.

"You're going to let Nathan get away with this? Like in the sermon?" asked Matthew.

"No," said Mr. Day. "I'll talk to Nathan's parents. Right now, I'm too angry. Sometimes, when I'm too upset, I like to pray about things before acting. I'll call the pastor when we get home. I'll invite him over tomorrow night. Then we'll talk things through."

"Can I stay home from school tomorrow? I'm afraid of what Nathan will do when he sees me," said Matthew.

"No," said Mr. Day.

"Then, can I have next week's allowance?" asked Matthew.

"Why?" asked Mr. Day.

"In case I have to bless Nathan to not hit me. One week's allowance just might cover it."

"Paying someone to not pick on you isn't the answer. I'll call the school and let them know about the problems Nathan is causing. By tomorrow night your little bullying problem will be solved. Just leave it to your good ol' dad."

Chapter 8

The Mystery Box

Matthew made it safely to class Monday morning. It didn't even cost him any of his allowance. He didn't even see Nathan until he got to the classroom. Matthew knew his father was going to call the school. The principal must have sent Nathan to the room so the teacher could keep an eye on him.

Matthew sat down. He noticed something on Rail's desk. His friend wasn't in class yet. On his desk was a box. Matthew recognized the box. He had one just like it. It was a Double Pump Slammers shoe box.

"Where did the box come from?" Matthew whispered to Buzz.

"I saw Nathan put it there," Buzz whispered back. "What do you think it is?"

"Uh…shoes I guess," said Matthew.

"I thought I was the funny one," said Buzz.

"What do you mean?" asked Matthew.

"It could be anything," said Buzz. "It has to

be a joke. I sure hope it doesn't hurt Rail. What would a bully put in a shoe box?"

Matthew was worried. He wasn't just worried that Rail might get scared. He would also be embarrassed. Everyone would laugh at him. Matthew knew things like that hurt Rail's feelings.

"We've got to get that box," said Matthew.

"But, Nathan will get mad if the box is missing," said Buzz.

The two boys thought for a moment. "I've got an idea," said Buzz. "I saw a box just like this one. Mr. Morgan was carrying it. We can sneak into his room. He has hall duty. We'll get his box and switch them."

Matthew smiled. He could just imagine the look on Nathan's face when his trick didn't work. Matthew and Buzz raised their hands. Mrs. Anderson was sitting at her desk.

"Yes boys?" asked Mrs. Anderson.

"Can I go to the restroom?" asked Matthew.

"Yes. Be back before class starts," said Mrs. Anderson.

Matthew and Buzz started to leave. "One at a time in the restroom," said Mrs. Anderson. "You know the rules."

"I don't need to use the restroom," said Buzz. "I need to check the lost and found."

"For what?" asked Mrs. Anderson.

"I'm not sure," said Buzz. "But, I think I lost something. I'll know it when I find it."

It wasn't one of Buzz's better excuses. He knew it. That's why he was surprised that Mrs. Anderson still let him go. Buzz was almost out the door when she stopped him.

"Oh, Bradley would you show Nathan to the office? He's this week's helper. You can show him where to turn in the lunch count."

Buzz didn't know what to say. Matthew was standing next to him by the door. Matthew poked him.

"That's perfect," whispered Matthew. "You keep Nathan busy while I switch the boxes."

"Can I go to the restroom for Matthew and let him show Nathan to the office?"

Mrs. Anderson laughed, "Quit joking around and go to the office with Nathan."

Buzz sighed. He glanced at Matthew. Matthew gave him a thumbs-up. Buzz started to shake his head no. It was too late. Nathan was walking to the door.

"It was nice knowing you," Buzz said to Matthew.

Matthew watched them walk down the hall and turn the corner. He then rushed to Mr. Morgan's room. The room was empty. The teacher was still on hall duty.

Matthew saw the Double Pump Slammers box and grabbed it. He hurried down the hall. Just then, he saw Mrs. Anderson. She came out of the room and turned the other way.

Matthew couldn't believe what she was carrying. Tucked under her arm was a Double Pump Slammers shoe box. Matthew ducked behind other students as he followed her. She stopped around a corner and talked to another teacher. Matthew crept closer so he could hear.

"I thought it would be best to wait until the assembly," Mrs. Anderson said to the other teacher. "I'm taking the box to the auditorium."

"Oh no!" thought Matthew. Rail would open the box in front of all the students. He was really going to be embarrassed. Matthew had to switch that box.

He followed Mrs. Anderson to the auditorium. Then, he hid in the boy's restroom. He waited until he heard her footsteps. She was going back to class.

Matthew stepped into the dark auditorium. There was the box. It was sitting on the stage. Matthew switched it with the one from Mr. Morgan's room. He hid Mrs. Anderson's box behind the tall curtain.

When he got back to class, Buzz and Nathan were in their seats. The bell rang just as Matthew stepped through the doorway. Buzz saw Matthew. He started to get up. He wanted to tell him something.

"Take your seats, boys," said Mrs. Anderson. "Class starts with the bell."

"Hey, there's a box on my desk," said Rail. He had just walked in the door.

Matthew turned and looked. He was shocked. The Double Pump Slammer shoebox was still on Rail's desk. There were three Double Pump Slammer boxes in school that day. Mrs. Anderson must have had her own box.

Matthew looked at Nathan. The giant third-grader had a huge grin on his face. Rail sat down. Matthew didn't have time to warn him.

He saw an open window. Matthew dashed for the box. In one smooth move he scooped it up and tossed it out the window. At last, Rail was safe.

"Matthew Day!" shouted Mrs. Anderson. "Why on earth would you do such a thing?"

"Uh…" Matthew didn't know how to explain it. "I was afraid it might explode?"

"Explode!" repeated Mrs. Anderson.

"Or bite?"

"Do your Double Pump Slammers explode and bite?" asked Mrs. Anderson.

"Double Pump Slammers! Is that what was in the box? How could I know?" Matthew tried to defend himself.

"Well," said Mrs. Anderson, "The box had Double Pump Slammers printed on it. That might have been a clue. Plus, you did help buy them."

"I bought them?" asked Matthew.

"Yes," said Mrs. Anderson. "Buzz, please go outside and get the shoes. Nathan, will you tell Rail what his friends did for him?"

"Yes, Mrs. Anderson," answered Nathan. "Rail, when you fell Friday I noticed your shoes were torn. That must be why you keep falling down. I was worried that you might get hurt. I asked Mrs. Anderson if I could collect money to buy you some new ones."

"So, at recess Friday, everyone chipped in. I was able to buy you Double Pump Slammers. They're the best you know. They even have the new sky blue soles. They're from all your friends. Even Matthew helped pay for them. I'm not sure why he threw them out the window."

Buzz came back with the shoes. Rail tried them on. They were perfect. All the students admired them.

"That was very thoughtful of Nathan," said Stacy.

Matthew looked at the girl with the black eye. He couldn't believe she could say something good about Nathan. It was hard to believe Nathan could do anything nice. Yet, there was Rail wearing brand-new Double Pump Slammers. It was all because of Nathan.

"Let's line up for the assembly," said Mrs. Anderson.

Chapter 9

Citizen of the Month

Several of the students wanted to sit next to Nathan at the assembly. Mrs. Anderson made him sit on the front row. Stacy sat next to him. Matthew sat three rows back. Buzz plopped down right next to Matthew.

"So what happened to Mr. Morgan's box?" asked Buzz.

"Oh no!" said Matthew. He saw the box on the stage. Mrs. Anderson picked it up. Matthew thought about diving for it. Then he remembered the shoes.

"What do you suppose is in it?" asked Buzz.

Mrs. Anderson held a microphone. "Good morning everyone. Welcome to our awards assembly." She motioned to Nathan and Stacy.

"We have an unusual citizen of the month. He's unusual because this student has only been with us three days."

"Nathan!" whispered Matthew. "He stole my lunchbox and he's citizen of the month?"

"Uh...about that," said Buzz. "When I was at lost and found, guess what I found."

"What?"

"Your Super Squid Master Detective lunchbox. It looks just like Nathan's. Only, it has your name on it...and week old lunch leftovers."

"My lunchbox? Then who's cupcake did I take last Friday?" asked Matthew.

"Nathan Goliath," said Mrs. Anderson. "Our citizen of the month! Stacy Lane was chased by a big dog on her way to school. She tripped and fell. Nathan drove the dog away with a stick. Then he helped her to school. Nathan is a real hero."

All the students clapped. Stacy sat down. Nathan started to follow her. But, Mrs.

Anderson stopped him.

"Our next award is for perfect attendance. As you know, we have a drawing for a prize. All the students who didn't miss a day for the last quarter can win. I have those names in a shoe box. Nathan will pull out our winner."

Mrs. Anderson held the shoe box above Nathan's head. Matthew covered his eyes. He couldn't watch. Nathan reached inside the box.

"Ahh!" yelled Nathan as he jumped back.

The startled Mrs. Anderson dropped the box. Something furry dashed out. The frightened animal slipped under the seats. Students all over the auditorium hopped up.

"It's a skunk!" someone shouted.

"It's a rat!" another student shouted.

Children were running out the doors. Everyone was panicking. Teachers were trying to keep their classes together. It was no use. The assembly was over.

Matthew wanted to run, too. Not away from the animal. He wanted to run and hide. Soon, nobody was left in the auditorium except Matthew.

The door opened. In walked Mr. Morgan. He was looking under the seats. He stopped in one row and started crawling.

"There you are," said Mr. Morgan. He stood up. In his arms was a fluffy little bunny. "Is my baby alright?"

"Your baby?" asked Matthew.

Mr. Morgan jumped. He hadn't seen Matthew.

"Uh…my bunny. I think I said my bunny." Then, he looked at Matthew. "You wouldn't know how my box ended up in the auditorium, would you?"

"Well…" Matthew had a long story to tell.

Mr. Morgan thought it would best be told in the office. The principal and Mr. Morgan listened to the whole thing. Matthew didn't know how much trouble he was in. Yet, a few times, the two men almost laughed. That was a good sign.

They called Nathan to the office. Matthew told him all about his misunderstandings. Matthew apologized. The giant third grader smiled. He stuck out his great big hand.

"Friends?" asked Nathan.

Matthew smiled, "Friends."

"That's great, boys," said Mr. Morgan. "Matthew, next time you have a problem at school, tell us. We're here to help you."

"So, I'm not in trouble?" asked Matthew.

"We didn't say that," answered the principal. "We've never quite had a problem like this. So, give us some time to think about it."

Matthew sighed. Nathan and Matthew left the office. The door closed behind them. Mr. Morgan and the principal roared with laughter. Nathan smiled.

"Can I sit next to you at lunch?" asked Nathan. "I brought you a cupcake."

"You brought me a cupcake?" asked Matthew. "Why?"

"I try to bless those who persecute me," smiled Nathan.

Matthew, Nathan, Rail, and the rest of the gang played baseball after school. It was a great game. Matthew made sure he didn't hit anyone with the baseball. He even cheered when Nathan hit a homerun off of his pitch.

After awhile, a car drove by the ballpark. Its horn honked. Nathan waved. Pastor Goliath waved back.

"Where's your dad going?" asked Matthew.

"Someone in the church asked if he could talk to him tonight."

Suddenly, Matthew remembered his dad. Matthew hadn't talked to his parents about Nathan. They still thought he was a bully. He had only been home long enough to get his baseball gear.

He hopped on his bike and raced home. The pastor's car was in the driveway. Matthew didn't know what he was going to do. He just knew he needed to stop his father.

The pastor was just getting out of the car. Matthew walked him to the door. He talked to

the pastor all the way.

"I'm so sorry I hit Nathan with the baseball. And, I'm sorry about the 'headless choir member' thing."

"Oh, that was you," said Nathan's dad. "Nathan knows the baseball was an accident. And, you did make my first church service here very interesting."

They reached the door. Mr. and Mrs. Day were waiting for them.

"Dad, this is Pastor Goliath. He's the father of the greatest third grader that ever lived."

Matthew's parents were puzzled. Did Nathan have a twin brother?

"Uh…the same third grader who tackled me yesterday?" asked Mr. Day as Matthew and Pastor Goliath stepped into the house.

"Oh, that was you," said Pastor Goliath. "I owe you a lot of thanks."

Mr. Day was now very confused. He expected an apology. Saying thanks for letting Nathan tackle him didn't make sense.

"Thanks for what?" asked Mr. Day.

"For catching Nathan when the tree swing broke," said Pastor Goliath. "Nathan thought he broke his arm. It was just a bruise. If you wouldn't have caught him, he could have been badly injured. When I came outside to see who helped him, you had left."

"Well, I care about the safety of children," beamed Mr. Day. "I didn't even think about sticking around to take the credit."

"That's true," said Matthew. "He wasn't thinking very well at all."

"Isn't that the tree swing you were supposed to fix?" Mrs. Day asked Mr. Day.

Mr. Day turned red. "Uh…yes," stammered Mr. Day.

"Well it turned out alright," said Pastor Goliath. "Now you said on the phone you wanted to talk about my sermon?"

Mr. Day didn't know what to say. Matthew

spoke up.

"Dad couldn't stop talking about your sermon Sunday. He had even told me the same thing the day before. The Bible says to bless those who persecute us.

We just want to say that you and Nathan have really blessed us. Still, we've decided to stop persecuting your family. We're so glad the Bible is true."

"I couldn't agree more," said Mr. Day.

"I'm feeling blessed already," smiled Pastor Goliath.

The Book of Matt is a chapter book series from McRuffy Press that emphasizes Christian values in a fresh and creative way.

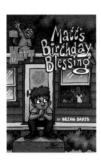

Matt's Birthday Blessing

Turning nine is just fine with Matthew Day. He's picked out a special birthday presnt, and knows how to get it. With God on his side, he can't go wrong. Or can he be?

ISBN 1-59269-056-4

My Shoes Got the Blues

What do a bulldog, a basketall star, and a big race have in common? They're all reasons Matthew's shoes have the blues. His Double Pump Slammers will never be the same.

ISBN 1-59269-057-2

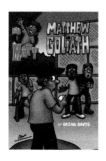

Matthew and Goliath

Big problems somtimes need small solutions. When Nathan Goliath moves to town, there's nothing but trouble, big trouble. Can one small boy stop the bullying?

ISBN 1-59269-058-0

About the author...

Brian Davis is a former school teacher. He has a Master's Degree in Reading instruction. He is the author of several reading, phonics, and math curricula, as well as other children's stories.

Brian and his wife, Sherylynn, have a daughter named Hannah, and a son named Matthew, who is sometimes, but not always, like the Matthew in the books.

About the illustrator...

You can find more of Ron Wheeler's work at his website: www.cartoonworks.com

Visit **www.McRuffy.com** for more
McRuffy Press products.

Find out the lastest about the Book of Matt at
www.TheBookofMatt.com